kindred

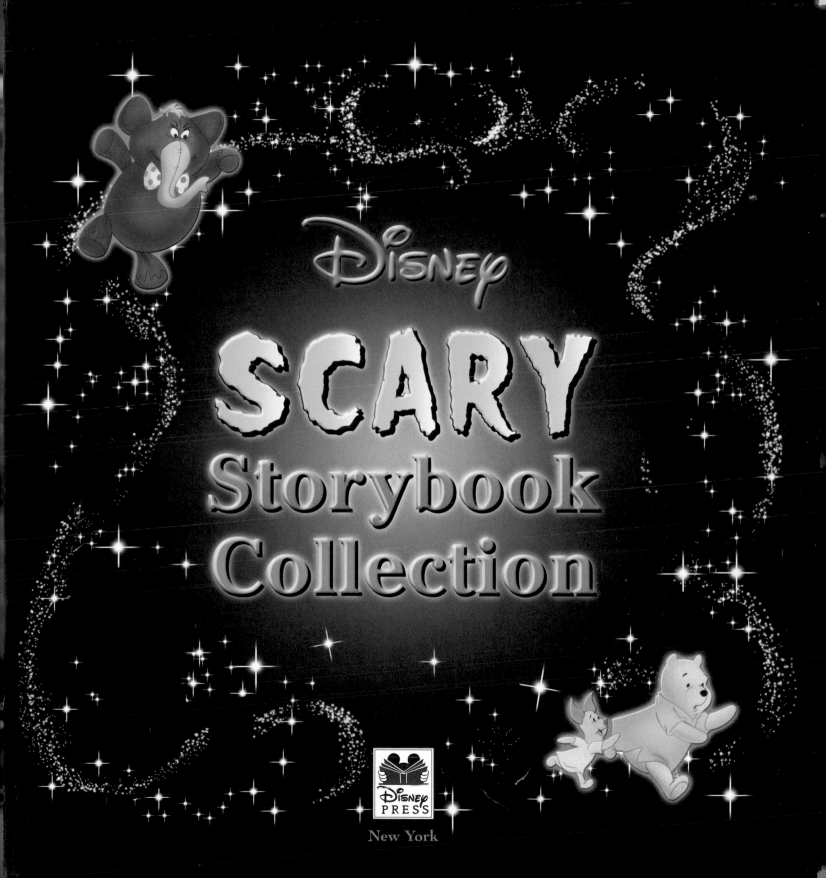

DISNEY

SCARY
Storybook
Collection

Disney
PRESS

New York

TABLE OF CONTENTS

TIM BURTON'S THE NIGHTMARE BEFORE CHRISTMAS
Jack's Story 5

WINNIE THE POOH
Frankenpooh 27

MICKEY AND FRIENDS
Haunted Halloween 47

THE ADVENTURES OF ICHABOD AND MR. TOAD
The Headless Horseman..69

WINNIE THE POOH
Pooh's Bad Dream 89

MICKEY MOUSE
Runaway Brain 111

WINNIE THE POOH
Boo to You, Winnie the Pooh! 131

DONALD DUCK
Donald Duck and the Witch Next Door...157

TABLE OF CONTENTS

ALADDIN
Who's That Ghost? 179

TARZAN®
One Brave Gorilla...199

PETER PAN
Captain Hook's Shadow 219

THE LITTLE MERMAID
The Sunken Ship..239

BEAUTY AND THE BEAST
The Haunted Castle 259

TOY STORY AND BEYOND!
Where's Woody? 279

MONSTERS, INC.
The Spooky Slumber Party..299

Designed by Alfred Giuliani

First Edition

1 3 5 7 9 10 8 6 4 2

This book is set in 20-point Cochin.

Library of Congress Catalog Card Number: 2002105294

ISBN: 0-7868-3379-3

For more Disney Press fun, visit www.disneybooks.com

TIM BURTON'S THE NIGHTMARE BEFORE CHRISTMAS

JACK'S STORY

Every year, on the last night of October, all the ghouls, ghosts, and goblins of Halloweentown went haunting. Always leading the way was Jack Skellington, the Pumpkin King.

Jack was the best. A wave of his bony hand could scare a grown man. His moans made heroes tremble. And yet, Jack was bored with it all. Every year, it's the same thing, Jack thought as he walked through the forest with his ghost dog Zero. Jack felt an emptiness in his bones.

Jack and Zero walked all night. Finally, they reached a grove of unusual trees. Jack had never been there before. One tree had a heart-shaped door. Another

had a shamrock. A third had a decorated egg. And a fourth had a turkey. But the one that caught Jack's eye had a strange tree painted on it. It was a Christmas tree.

Jack opened the door. In a flash, he was sucked down the tree and soon found himself sitting in a snowbank . . . in Christmastown! Every tree around him was a Christmas tree. Every house glowed with colored lights. There were toys and mistletoe and snowflakes everywhere.

Despite the cold, Jack's heart felt warm.

Jack raced back to Halloweentown, a huge grin spreading across his skull. At Town Hall, the ghouls all gathered around to hear what Jack had to say.

Jack started to explain about Christmas—the presents, the Christmas tree with lights, and the stockings filled with toys.

All the ghouls had lots of questions for Jack. They were especially interested in the toys, and wanted to know if they snapped, bit, or exploded.

But no one really understood.

Except Sally. Sally liked Jack better than anyone. She believed in him. But she didn't like his idea of Halloweentown's trying out this Christmas thing. It sounded like trouble.

Jack decided to study up on Christmas to find out what it was all about. He read every Christmas book he could find. He squished a holly berry to see what was inside. He stripped a candy cane of its stripes. He even

pulled the stuffing from a teddy bear and crushed a Christmas ball. But still he didn't know what it all meant.

Jack stayed in his tower for days. He finally came out when he realized that there was no reason why he couldn't handle Christmas. In fact, he thought he could make it even better!

Jack gave everyone a job. The vampires made toys. Sally sewed a red Santa suit for him. And three ghouls named Lock, Shock, and

Barrel had the most important task of all—they had to kidnap Santa Claus so Jack could take his place.

Soon it was Christmas Eve. Sally gave Jack the Santa suit to put on.

"You don't look like yourself, Jack," Sally said sadly.

"Isn't that wonderful?" Jack said.

Jack climbed into his sleigh. He gave a signal to
his skeleton reindeer. And with Zero leading the way,
the reindeer pulled the sleigh up into the sky.

Jack landed at the first house in Christmastown. A little boy named Timmie heard him come down the chimney.

"Santa!" the boy shouted.

Jack grinned his biggest grin as he handed a present to Timmie. The boy opened the box. Inside was a shrunken head!

Timmie screamed.

"Merry Christmas!" said Jack.

Jack traveled from rooftop to rooftop. At every house, he left behind tricks, not treats—a killer wreath, an evil wooden duckie, a biting doll. . . . The screams followed him through Christmastown.

To Jack, the screams meant happiness. He didn't know any better because that's what they meant in Halloweentown.

But the people of Christmastown weren't happy. They called the police. The police called the army. And the army launched its missiles into the sky to shoot down the mysterious skeleton in the sleigh.

"Santa! Come back and save Christmas!" cried the townspeople. They had no idea that Santa was in no position to do that.

Meanwhile, Lock, Shock, and Barrel had taken Santa to Oogie Boogie's dungeon. Oogie Boogie was the most foul and evil creature in all of Halloweentown.

Jack's friend Sally was Santa's only hope. She was trying to fix all of Jack's mistakes.

"I'll get you out of here," Sally whispered to Santa. She tricked Oogie Boogie into looking the other way, and then she untied Santa. But just as the two were escaping, Oogie turned around. In an instant, Sally and Santa were once again taken captive!

Meanwhile, high in the sky over Christmastown, missiles streaked by Jack's sleigh. Jack smiled.

"They're thanking us!" he said.

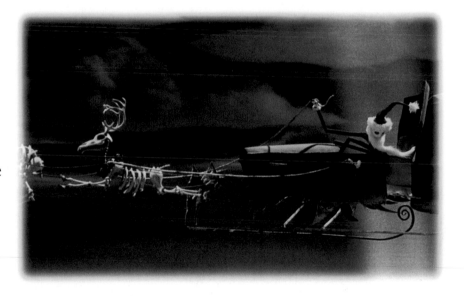

Then a missile hit one of Jack's reindeer. Jack's smile disappeared. "They're trying to hit us!" he cried.

Suddenly, a missile hit the sleigh, and it broke into pieces. Jack and Zero tumbled toward the ground.

The terrible news about Jack's sleigh being blown to smithereens reached Oogie Boogie's dungeon.

Sally gasped.

Oogie laughed.

He grabbed a lever, and the table Santa and Sally were tied to tilted over a vat of boiling stew. They slid down the table. But when Oogie didn't hear a splash, he pulled the table back.

Jack's smiling face greeted him!

Jack had survived the crash, and it had knocked some sense into him. He wasn't Santa Claus. He was the Pumpkin King!

Jack knew he had to set things right. So he headed to Oogie's to find Santa Claus.

"J-J-Jack, but they said you were dead!" Oogie cried.

First, Oogie Boogie tried to capture Jack, but Jack was too quick. Then Oogie tried to escape. Jack tugged on a string hanging from Oogie's body—and Oogie started to unravel! He was made entirely of bugs, spiders, and snakes!

"My bugs!" Oogie wailed, as the creepy-crawlies

began escaping. Soon, there was nothing left of Oogie.

Jack apologized to Santa. And Santa, being Santa, forgave him. Then Santa lifted a finger, and in the blink of an eye he was gone. He still had to fix Christmas!

Soon after, Sally left Oogie's dungeon. Jack followed her to the cemetery. Finally, she stopped at the top of Spiral Hill. Jack stood next to her.

Jack had finally realized what would fill the empty place in his heart. It was Sally—his dearest friend.

Sally held her hand out to Jack. He took it. Far above them, a Christmas star twinkled brightly in the sky.

Disney

Winnie the Pooh

FRANKENPOOH

It was the sort of crisp and sparkling autumn afternoon in the Hundred-Acre Wood that filled the heart of a very small animal with a story bursting to be told and desperate to be listened to.

And, at Piglet's house, where he had just finished hosting a small tea for his friends Rabbit, Pooh, Tigger, and Gopher, Piglet quietly announced that telling a story was just what he was going to do!

Tigger leaped out of the overstuffed armchair he was sharing with Rabbit and Gopher to where Piglet was standing nervously on the hearth.

"Is it a ghost story full o' spookables an' horribibble creatures? Or," said Tigger with a gasp, "is it about a MAD-scientist type?"

"Oh no!" Piglet protested. "Not mad at all! Quite happy and cheerful, really." Then he began the story. "Once upon a time . . ."

Tigger listened for a moment, then interrupted. "Say, it's broad daylight! Even a not-so-scary story has to happen at night, ya know!"

The picture in Piglet's head of a beautiful castle on a bright summer's day suddenly grew very dark. "Oh dear," he said to himself.

"An'," said Tigger, "a nice thunderstorm wouldn't hurt, either!"

Piglet's ears drooped as his imagination included a fierce thunderstorm crashing and rattling around the castle in his story.

But Piglet wasn't ready to give up. He had a story to tell and he was going to tell it his way, if no one minded very much.

Piglet thought about what glorious snacks he could whip up in a spotlessly neat and busily buzzing laboratory if he were a pleasant and very cheerful scientist. He wasn't a bit mad. He wasn't even slightly annoyed. Not even at Tigger.

"Mmm," Piglet said as he imagined the scientist holding a dripping sandwich. "Peanut butter and jelly. My favorite. And so very good for you, too!"

Then Tigger suddenly gasped, interrupting Piglet's story.

"What is it?" Piglet said demandingly. "What is it?"

"If you're gonna tell a story about a scientist," Tigger said, "he ought to at least be doin' somethin' terribibble, like creatin' a boogly, boogly MONSTER!"

"A monster?" Piglet said in a tiny, not-very-hopeful-that-the-story-was-going-to-go-his-way sort of voice.

"Yeah!" said Tigger. "The monster . . . FRANKENPOOH!"

The scientist looked at
Frankenpooh with mixed feelings.
Pooh? A
MONSTER?

"Yeah!"
Tigger said. "That's absoposilutely perfect. Only he oughta
be bigger than that!"

And at once Frankenpooh grew bigger! And bigger and
bigger until the very small scientist felt very small indeed!

"Oh bother," said Frankenpooh with a sigh as he
bumped his head on the top of the page.

"Now *that's* what I call a monster," Tigger said with satisfaction. "Hoo-hoo-hoo!"

The very small scientist ran around the monster's feet in a frightened flurry of activity, shouting, "Oh help me! Oh save me!"

"This is very terrorfryin'," Tigger said in delight.

The monster Frankenpooh, after much think-think-thinking and scratching of his oversized ears, reached a monstrous conclusion.

"I want . . . honey?" he said in a voice so loud he surprised himself.

And he went looking for a not-so-small smackerel of something sweet to eat.

"Honey!" he said again, just because he liked the sound of it.

"And the monster Frankenpooh," said Tigger, "went lookin' high and low for whatever it is monster Frankenpoohs look for."

"Honey!" yelled Frankenpooh again.

"An' the villagers skedaddled for life and lumber," Tigger said. "Trembling in your socks, aren't ya? Clinging to the edge of your seats? But there's no stoppin' the gigantical monstrous monstrosity!

"An' everybody was up to their necks in arms," Tigger continued dramatically, "because they knew who it was that was responsibibble for the horribibblest monster that was terrorfryin' them."

"Oh d-d-dear," said the scientist with a moan as he found himself surrounded by the full-of-wrath villagers.

"Help!" said the scientist. "Stop the story! Please! It was an accident! I didn't mean to do it! I just wanted it to be a nice, not-so-scary story."

And Piglet opened his eyes to discover himself back on the hearth of his very own fireplace, surrounded by his good friends Tigger, Rabbit, and Gopher.

"But, Piglet," said Tigger, "it was nothin' to get so upset about."

"It was just a s-s-silly story," whistled Gopher.

"Of course, Piglet," said Rabbit gently. "There was no monster. And no one's angry at you."

Piglet looked around in great relief. "No?" he asked in a small voice.

"No," all his friends said reassuringly.

After his friends had settled Piglet in his favorite
armchair and given him a cup of his favorite hot
chocolate, Rabbit put his arm comfortingly around Piglet's
very small shoulder.

"You really should learn the difference between what's
real and what
isn't," Rabbit
said gently
to Piglet.
"Shouldn't he,
POOH?"

"Yes, Piglet," said the very large and Frankenpooh-looking bear, "you really should. And so should I."

Then he emitted quite the largest Pooh Bear sort of sigh they had ever heard.

"Oh bother."

And Pooh did eventually get the story straightened

out in his head full of fluff, and returned to the

convenient size

proper to the

amounts

of honey

required

to feed

an always

hungry bear.

Walt Disney's

MICKEY AND FRIENDS

HAUNTED HALLOWEEN

"I am going to have a really terrific Halloween party tonight," Mickey said to himself. "If I ever finish getting ready!"

Mickey tacked one last fake cobweb to the wall. "Now it's time

to make the popcorn balls," he said.

An hour later, Mickey looked around his spooky living room.

"Everything seems great!" he said happily.

Mickey glanced at the clock. "Golly!" he said. "It's almost time for the party, and I haven't put my costume together yet!"

Mickey knew he had an old pirate costume tucked away in the attic.

"Now just where did I put that costume?" Mickey asked.

Up, up a creaky ladder he headed, into the dark attic. As soon as he switched on the light, thunder crashed outdoors.

Lightning flashed across the sky. Then out went the attic light!

"Oh, dear!" Mickey said as he stumbled around in the dark. Just then he blundered into a huge cobweb.

"Yikes!" he said with a shudder. "These spiderwebs are all over the place!"

Luckily, the light quickly came back on again.

"Thank goodness," Mickey said. "Aa-aaa-choo! There's an awful lot of dust up here!"

Finally, Mickey found the old trunk he'd been looking for.

"Achoo!" Mickey sneezed again. "I'll bet my pirate costume's in here." Mickey turned the key in the rusty old lock, and the trunk popped open.

"AAAGHH!"
Mickey shouted.
A skeleton
grinned up at
him! Then
Mickey realized
that it was just a
plastic party decoration.

"Whew!" he said in relief. "What a
good Halloween joke on me! This skeleton will be
perfect for my party! I'd better take the whole trunk

downstairs," Mickey said as he rummaged through it. "There's a lot of cool Halloween stuff in here!"

Meanwhile, in Mickey's backyard, Pluto had been chasing a ball through the sheets hanging on the clothesline. As Pluto

charged under one

of the sheets,

it came loose

from the line

and fell on

top of him. It

covered him

from head to tail.

Suddenly, rain
began to fall.
The wet
sheet stuck
to Pluto
like glue.
No matter
how hard
he tried, he
couldn't shake it
off. And he couldn't see anything, either!

It really began to pour as Donald, Goofy, Minnie, and Daisy drove up to Mickey's house.

"Gawrsh! Look at the lightning!" Goofy exclaimed.

"It's a spooky Halloween night," said Daisy with a nervous giggle.

"Let's run right into the house," said Minnie. "If we wait for Mickey to answer the door, our costumes will get soaked."

BOOM! went the thunder as Mickey's friends hurried into his house.

"Mickey, we're here!" called Minnie. "Where are you?"

But Mickey didn't answer. He was still in the attic, too far upstairs to hear anything over the sounds of the storm.

Just then, the lights went out again!

"Uh-oh!" said Donald.

THUM-KA-THUMP-THUMP! Weird, bumping

sounds were coming from somewhere above their heads.

"Wh-what was that?" Minnie said with a gasp.

Then they heard something big and heavy being slowly lugged across the floor upstairs!

"It—it sounds like a coffin being dragged across Mickey's room!" whispered Goofy.

Meanwhile, in the backyard, poor Pluto was still stuck

under the sheet. He couldn't see to find his doggie door.

"Aaaarrr! Arr! Arr!" Pluto howled.

"What's that sound?" Daisy whispered.

"Shh! Shhhh!" Goofy whispered back.

Just then, something weird and white ran past the window.

"It's a g-g-ghost!" exclaimed Daisy.

Mickey's friends were too scared even to scream!

Meanwhile, up in the attic, Mickey lit a candle and changed into his costume. Then, picking up the skeleton decoration, he slowly and carefully headed down the dark staircase. Mickey's friends heard a slow shuffling of feet and a rattling of bones. They looked up to see a horrible monster coming toward them. This time,

everybody screamed!

Suddenly, the

lights came back on.

"Hi, everybody,"

Mickey said with

surprise. "You really

scared me!"

"Oh, Mickey! It's

just you!" cried

Minnie. "You really scared *us*!"

"That's one scary costume!" Donald said with a shiver.

Daisy picked up a cupcake and began to munch. "Mickey," she said, "this is the scariest, most exciting Halloween ever! How did you do it?"

"Gawrsh, Mickey, it's the best haunted house I've ever been in," added Goofy.

"Er— haunted house?" said a puzzled Mickey, looking around.

Just then,
Pluto finally
found his way
in through the
doggie door. He
happily galloped

into the living room. Mickey and his friends looked up

and saw—a ghost! And, boy, did they scream.

"Arf!" barked Pluto.

"Oh, Pluto! It's just you!" said Mickey in relief. "Hey,

boy, you're all wet! Let's get you dried off!"

"You're right," Mickey told his friends with a laugh, as he dried Pluto with a towel. "This *is* the scariest Halloween ever!"

Walt Disney's

The Adventures of Ichabod and Mr. Toad

THE HEADLESS HORSEMAN

Ichabod Crane was a schoolmaster who lived in Sleepy Hollow. He was tall and lanky, and looked like a scarecrow.

Ichabod read books all day. He read all kinds of stories, except scary ones. Ichabod didn't like spooky tales, because he believed that ghosts and goblins were real.

One Halloween night, Ichabod went to a party. There was music and dancing. Then  Old Man Van Tassel asked if any of his guests would tell a ghost story.

"I know one," Brom Bones said. He was famous in Sleepy Hollow for his creepy stories. "But it may be too

frightening for *some* people."

Ichabod gulped. He did not like to hear scary stories at all.

But Old Man Van Tassel insisted that Brom tell his tale.

"After all, it's Halloween," Old Man Van Tassel said. So Brom cleared his throat and began his story:

His story was about a headless horseman who rode out into the hollow every Halloween night, scarching for a new head to replace his flaming pumpkin head.

"The only way to escape the Headless Horseman is to cross the bridge over the brook," Brom said. "That's where his power ends."

Ichabod nodded fearfully, thinking that if he ever ran into the Headless Horseman, he would remember what Brom had said and ride straight for the bridge.

Soon the party was over. Ichabod said good night to everyone, and climbed onto his horse.

While Ichabod rode toward the hollow, the sky seemed to grow darker and darker as clouds covered the moon and stars.

A cold breeze blew through the air. It sent a chill through the schoolmaster and made the trees groan above him.

As Ichabod rode farther into the murky hollow, he began to feel very frightened. The forest seemed to

close in behind him, and Ichabod began to remember Brom's story, word for word. Tonight is Halloween, the school-master thought. The Headless Horseman could be close by!

Ichabod covered his eyes, but he couldn't get rid of the image of the Headless Horseman that lurked in his mind.

All around him, strange voices seemed to whisper Ichabod's name, telling him to beware. Ichabod would have turned and run away, but this was the only way home.

The wind howled through the trees, bending their branches like long arms that reached for the schoolmaster. Suddenly, a bough above him broke. The limb crashed down—falling straight toward Ichabod!

Ichabod screamed, and his horse leaped forward. Branches clawed at the schoolmaster's face. He batted them away, but then he plunged into a huge spiderweb. Ichabod tried to clear the web away, but it covered his eyes— he couldn't see.

When Ichabod finally managed to see clearly again, he got back on his horse. But all the schoolmaster could hear was the hollow *clop-clop* of horse's hooves as he rode through the woods.

As Ichabod looked around, he noticed that they seemed to be riding very slowly—in fact, the trees didn't seem to be getting any farther away.

That's when Ichabod realized that he wasn't moving at all. So,

he tried pushing the horse. Then he tried pulling the horse. But the horse wouldn't budge.

But where was that sound coming from?

Could it be . . . the Headless Horseman? The sound was getting louder now, and Ichabod grew more

frightened with each echoing clop.

Ichabod looked around and discovered that the sound was coming from some cattails that were knocking against a hollow log by his side. Ichabod was so relieved that he started to laugh.

Just then, someone else laughed, too!

It was the Headless Horseman! He was real, after all! The Headless Horseman rode toward Ichabod, a gleaming sword in his hand! The schoolmaster climbed back onto his horse and grabbed the reins. He had to get away as fast as he could!

Ichabod screamed and turned his horse around. He had to make it across the bridge! But the Headless Horseman was close behind, his sharp sword shining in the moonlight.

The schoolmaster could see the bridge in the distance — but at the same time he could hear the sound of the

Headless Horseman gaining on him.

Ichabod urged his horse to go faster. He was almost at the bridge. The Headless Horseman swiped at the schoolmaster with his sword.

He wants a new head! Ichabod thought to himself. Ichabod kicked at his horse, which sprang forward with a burst of speed.

But at the foot of the bridge, Ichabod's horse slipped in a mud puddle, and spun around.

Now, Ichabod was facing the Headless Horseman. He could see down the horseman's collar. And there was nothing inside at all!

The horseman lunged at Ichabod, who screamed and turned toward the bridge. He was almost at the other side when the Headless Horseman reared his horse and threw his pumpkin head at the schoolmaster. The pumpkin was lit with a fire from within, and Ichabod cried out as it came toward him. . . .

The next morning, Ichabod's hat was found beside a shattered pumpkin. But Ichabod was nowhere to be found.

Some people said that he had run away and married a rich widow in a distant county.

But, of course, the people of Sleepy Hollow always believed that the schoolmaster had been taken by the Headless Horseman!

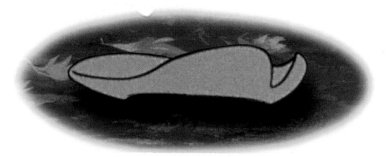

Winnie the Pooh

Pooh's Bad Dream

Winnie the Pooh stood back and admired his work. "Ten new pots of honey," he said, sighing heavily.

"Very nice," said Tigger. "Just make sure that horrible heffalump doesn't eat them tonight."

"The horrible heffalump?" Pooh said.

"He's a greedy gobbler!" said Tigger.

"You've seen him?" asked Pooh.

"No," said Tigger, "but it's even worse when you don't see him. You can't be too careful when a heffalump's sneaking around."

"I'll be careful," said Pooh.

"Worraworow," growled Tigger bravely. "T-T-F-N—Ta-Ta-For-Now!"

Pooh locked his door. His house seemed big and empty.

Pooh climbed into bed and pulled the quilt over his nose. And he stayed that way for a long time.

"Horrible heffalump," he said to himself. "Must keep watch. . . ." He watched and he watched and he watched, until he couldn't keep his eyes open any longer.

Then, suddenly, his house shook like thunder. A big red heffalump crashed through the door. He broke dishes and toppled the lamps. He stomped over to Pooh's cupboard and guzzled three pots of honey.

"Oh!" cried Pooh.

The heffalump turned and looked at Pooh with his horrible green eyes. He snuffled him with his long blue snout.

"Ho-ho!" he said. "Now I'm going to eat you!"

The heffalump scrunched a honeypot down over Pooh's head.

"Mmppfh!" cried Pooh.

He jumped out of bed. He reached up to pull the pot off his head, but . . . the pot was gone. The heffalump was gone, too.

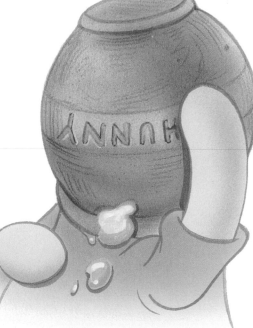

"Where is he hiding?" Pooh said. He was afraid to look.

Pooh ran to Piglet's house as fast as he could.

"Help, Help! A ho-horrible heffalump is ha-hiding in my huh-house," said Pooh.

"A huh? A heff? A who?" stammered Piglet, rubbing his eyes.

"A heffalump. Hurry!" cried Pooh.

Piglet had no time to think. If he had had time to think, he certainly would not be rushing to Pooh's house in the night to help him find a horrible heffalump.

"Come out, heffalump!" Pooh cried, opening the door.

Piglet grabbed Pooh's broom and held it over his head.

"Pooh?" asked Piglet, who finally had time to think. "What will we do with the heffalump when we find him?"

Pooh thought and thought and thought.

"Maybe we should go get Christopher Robin,"
said Piglet.

"Good thinking," said Pooh.

Christopher Robin was in bed when they arrived.

"Poor Pooh," he said. "You must have had a bad dream.

Heffalumps aren't real."

"He *was* real,"

said Pooh. "I felt

him snuffle me

with his blue

snout. He said

he was going

to eat me!"

"If there is a heffalump in your house, then Piglet and I will help you find him," said Christopher Robin stoutly.

"We will? I-I mean, yes, we will," said Piglet.

Together they mounted an expedition to find the
horrible heffalump and chase him from Pooh's house
forever. They looked under Pooh's bed. They searched

behind his

mirror.

They

lifted the

tablecloth

and peered

under the

table.

They opened his cupboard. All ten pots stood side by side, just as Pooh had left them.

Pooh scratched behind his ear. "It must have been a dream. But why did it seem so real?" he asked.

"Dreams can seem real," said Christopher Robin. "But they happen only in your mind."

"Oh," said Pooh. "But if I was asleep, how could my mind be making up a heffalump?"

"Every night, when your body sleeps, your brain stays awake part of the time," said Christopher Robin.

"That's when you are dreaming!" cried Piglet.

"Right!" said Christopher Robin. "Usually dreams are nice—and you forget them as soon as you wake up. But if you're especially tired or worried about something, then sometimes a dream turns into a bad dream, or a nightmare."

"I was a little worried," said Pooh, thinking of what Tigger had said earlier. "And I'm so sleepy. But . . ."

Piglet tucked Pooh into bed.

". . . what if my brain brings the heffalump back?" asked Pooh.

"It's your dream," said Christopher Robin. "And

you're in charge. If the heffalump comes back, just look him in the eye and say: 'Heffalump—go away!'"

"Heffalump, go away . . . Heff . . . go. . . ." Pooh said repeatedly until he was fast asleep.

Piglet and Christopher Robin tiptoed out.

Then, suddenly, Pooh's house shook like thunder. A big red heffalump stomped right up to Pooh's bed!

"Ho-ho!" he boomed.

"Heffalump, ga-wah . . . H-Hurrfa . . . lumph, hahh!" cried Pooh.

The heffalump was confused. "What?" he asked.

"Go away," said Pooh huskily.

The heffalump stopped. His lip began to tremble.

Tears came to his eyes.

"What's wrong?" asked Pooh.

"I just wanted a little snack, that's all," said the

heffalump, "and now—*sniff*—you're sending me away?"

Pooh began to feel sorry that he had been so rough

with the heffalump.

"I'm feeling a bit

rumbly in my tumbly,

too," he said. "Would

you like to share a pot

of honey?"

The big heffalump looked rather silly sitting in Pooh's little chair. But he didn't seem to mind.

This time, Pooh and the heffalump dreamed a sweet dream together.

Disney's

MICKEY MOUSE

Runaway Brain

I t was a dark, stormy night. Thunder crashed as a bolt of lightning lit up the sky. Mickey

Mouse stood in front of his television set. He was playing one of his favorite video games.

"I'm gonna finish 'em off! Take that and that!" Mickey yelled at the screen, punching the buttons on his controller. "Catch one of these!"

Mickey's excitement was contagious. His faithful dog, Pluto, raced around the room barking up a storm. Just then, the doorbell rang, but Mickey was so absorbed in the game, he didn't even hear it.

"Mickey? Hello?" called out a high voice. It was Mickey's longtime girlfriend, Minnie Mouse.

Minnie planted herself in front of the TV screen and began chattering excitedly. It was a very special night—the  anniversary of Mickey and Minnie's very first date. Unfortunately, Mickey had forgotten all about it.

"Minnie! You tryin' to get me killed?" Mickey cried, diving past Minnie so he could see the screen and defend himself against the video villains.

Minnie's smile faded. How could Mickey forget the most romantic day of their lives? It was unthinkable!

"Ooooh! Well, from now on you can date your stupid video games!" Minnie said in a huff.

Uh-oh, thought Mickey. He hated to upset Minnie. He had to think of a way to set things right.

Just then, Mickey spotted an ad in the newspaper. It was for a free game of miniature golf. "I've got everything planned. You see, I was saving it for a surprise," he told Minnie, holding up the paper. "Ta-da!"

Reluctantly, Minnie peeked at the paper. She saw an ad, but it wasn't for miniature golf. It was for a

Hawaiian cruise. Minnie thought Mickey was taking her on an exotic vacation!

"Oh, Mickey! You're so sweet," she gushed, giving him a kiss and skipping out the door.

Mickey's jaw hit the ground when he realized what had happened. He couldn't disappoint Minnie. But how

would he pay for a Hawaiian cruise?

Luckily, Pluto had an idea. He brought Mickey the want ads.

"'Earn $999.99 for a mindless day's work,'" read Mickey. "Oh, boy! I'm back in business!"

With his newspaper in hand, Mickey went in search of the address, 1313 Lobotomy Lane. It wasn't long before he reached a tall, dark building. "This is it!" said Mickey, double-checking the address in the paper. He quickly slipped on a tie, and rang the doorbell. Suddenly, Mickey fell through a trapdoor in the front step!

Down, down, down Mickey tumbled through a long dark chute. Finally, he landed in a chair. *SNAP!* A metal clamp closed over his left arm. *SNAP!* Another one closed over his right arm. Mickey looked around. He was in some kind of strange laboratory.

Just then, a mad scientist in a lab coat swung down from the rafters, staring at Mickey. "Dr. Frankenollie, at your service," he said in a raspy voice. "You're here for the job, hmm?"

"Yeah . . . I mean, no," Mickey said. He gulped. This wasn't exactly the job he had in mind. But Dr. Frankenollie wouldn't take no for an answer.

"Let me introduce your coworker," the doctor said, hitting a switch. "I made him myself."

Within minutes, an enormous, snarling monster emerged from a hole in the floor.

"Yaaaah!" Mickey screamed.

The doctor stuck a helmet on Mickey's head.

"Julius, Julius, baby," Dr. Frankenollie said to the

monster. "Daddy's found you a brand-new brain!"

Mickey couldn't believe his ears! Dr. Frankenollie was going to put *his* brain in the *monster's* body! Suddenly, the doctor pulled a lever. *ZAP!* Sparks flew through the air.

"Omigosh, I'm not myself," said Mickey after the dust settled. His brain was in the body of the monster! And the monster's brain was in Mickey's body!

"That crazy gizmo really worked!" cried Mickey.

He tried to explain everything to the monster.

"Uh, you, monster . . . me, Mickey Mouse," he said, pulling out his wallet and pointing. "There's me next to my girlfriend, Minnie!"

The monster fell in love with the picture of Minnie. "Minnie . . . Minnie," he chanted, escaping from the lab.

Meanwhile, in a surf shop downtown, Minnie flipped through racks of colorful bathing suits, searching for the perfect suit to wear on the cruise to Hawaii.

Just then, the monster (in Mickey's body) crashed through the front door of the store. Mickey (in the monster's body) followed close on his heels.

With a shriek, Minnie began pelting Mickey with a flipper. Then she pulled the monster outside. She didn't realize that the *real* Mickey was stuck in the monster's body! Minnie and the monster started to run.

Suddenly, Mickey drove by in a bus. He grabbed Minnie's hand and pulled her on board. "Minnie, stop! It's me, Mickey," he said.

As they drove through a construction site, Mickey explained what had happened. Then Mickey and Minnie jumped off the bus. They were able to swing to the top of a building on a crane. Then Mickey went to battle with the monster.

Seconds later, an electrical explosion lit up the sky. While fighting, Mickey and the monster had tumbled onto a power line! The shock switched back their brains.

Now, Mickey had his body back and Minnie by his side. But there was one problem. The monster had

crashed

into a giant

billboard

and was

holding

Mickey in

one hand and Minnie in the other.

"*Rarrgh!*" roared the monster and he broke through the billboard.

Mickey knew that he had to save Minnie and himself. So, he chomped down on the monster's hand. As Minnie watched in horror, the monster flung Mickey off the edge of the building! Luckily, Mickey landed safely on a window washer's platform. Then, grabbing some rope, Mickey quickly tied up the monster.

"Oh, Mickey," said Minnie with a sigh.

Later that day, Mickey and Minnie set sail for Hawaii. The cruise didn't cost Mickey one penny— that's because the monster towed them the whole way!

"You're so romantic," Minnie said, giving Mickey a great big kiss. This was one anniversary Mickey would never forget!

Disney

Winnie the Pooh

BOO TO YOU, WINNIE THE POOH!

Once each year, as October breezes puff and bluster, there comes a most particular and most peculiar night, when the dark grows a little more so, and the trees jitter and rattle their leaves until they chatter like frightened teeth. And on this particular and peculiar night, Winnie the Pooh was dressed as a giant

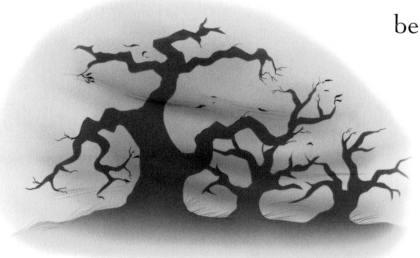

bee and pouring the contents of a large pot of honey into his mouth.

"Practicing for

Halloween," he said with a chuckle between gulps. "Though I'm not fond of tricking, I do enjoy the treating . . . especially of myself."

Just as Pooh was savoring the last smackerel of sweetness, a creature in baggy pajamas with a skeleton painted on them bounced on him.

"Not late, am I?" asked Tigger, for, of course, that was who the bouncer was. Behind Tigger were *two* Eeyores—one wrapped in bandages like a mummy, and the other a sort of bedraggled, Eeyore-like creature.

"Hello, Eeyore," said Pooh to the mummified donkey. "And, hello, Gopher," he said to the other Eeyore.

"Ding-dagnabbit!" said Gopher. "How am I supposed to win the best-costume contest if you know it's *me*!"

"C'mon, Pooh!" cried Tigger. "We'd better get a move on!"

"Not," Pooh said, "until our good friend Piglet joins us."

Meanwhile, strange things were happening at Piglet's house. Crouched in the middle of his parlor was the most horrible pretend spookable costume that the very small animal could put together.

"If I'm not scared of something as frightful as this," Piglet said, "I won't be afraid of anything this Halloween."

At that moment, the front door was flung open and Piglet was joyfully bounced on by Tigger the skeleton.

"Boo-hoo-hoo!" shouted Tigger.

"Why, Piglet," said the surprised Pooh, "where's your costume?"

"Yeah, look at the time," said Tigger. "It's half past a quarter to sunset! We gotta get to Halloweenin'!"

"Oh . . . uh . . . I . . ." Piglet said, stammering.

"And while Piglet is figuring out what he will be this Halloween," said Pooh, "I think I should try out my costume by tricking a small smackerel of something sweet from our friends at the honey tree."

"But, Pooh—" Piglet said.

"Perhaps it would be best," Pooh said, "if you didn't call me by my given name. It might make the bees suspicious."

"Enough jabberin'," said Tigger. "Let's get to terrorfyin'!"

So, much to Piglet's distress, they followed Pooh.

But they were on their way back almost immediately, running as fast as they could, with a blizzard of angry, buzzing bees close behind!

Not too far down the path, Rabbit was in the middle of his pumpkin patch, his chest swelling with pride as he stepped from one pumpkin to another.

The sudden approach of a buzzing noise caused Rabbit to look up, but there was no time for him to utter a word as Pooh, Piglet, Tigger, and Eeyore crashed past him, tumbling into the patch.

The bees, seeing Rabbit standing still, swarmed at him in a humming hurricane of anger. At that very last instant, Rabbit realized he was in danger and ducked! The bees swooped over his head and between his ears, into the knothole of a tree behind him. The resourceful Rabbit quickly covered the hole with a bucket, trapping the belligerent bees inside.

Rabbit then surveyed the state of his pumpkins and his friends and shook his head in exasperation. "Of all my favorite holidays," he said with a sigh, "Halloween isn't one!"

Very soon, night fell and Halloween officially arrived— along with a storm. Everyone hurried home.

At his house, Piglet scurried around, frantically blocking his front door with furniture. All about were posted signs that read SPOOKABLES—SCRAM! And NO GHOSTS ALLOWED! And GOBLINS, GO HOME!

So, when a knock sounded at his front door, Piglet was not at all eager to answer it.

"Who . . . who's there?" he squeaked, keeping his hands over his eyes.

"It's me . . . them . . . us!" said

a very Pooh-sounding voice.

"Pooh Bear?" said Piglet. "How can I be certain it's really you? Perhaps if you say something only you would say, then I'd be certain. How about 'I am Pooh'?"

"You are?" said the now totally confused Pooh. "Then, who am I?"

"Pooh Bear!" squealed Piglet as he opened the door to reveal Pooh, Tigger, and Eeyore.

"Piglet," said Pooh, "will you be joining us for Halloween?"

"I'm afraid I'm just really too afraid," Piglet said nervously.

"That's quite all right," said Pooh Bear. "We'll simply not have Halloween. This Halloween shall be a Hallo*wasn't*."

"Thank you, Pooh Bear," Piglet said, smiling.

Later that night, the storm began to rage fiercely.

Pooh watched it from his window and frowned.

"I hope Piglet is not too frightened," he said. "He is, of course, all alone."

Gazing out of his window, Pooh said, "I suspect that something should be done. But what?"

He concentrated fiercely. "Think-think-*think*!" he

muttered. And, to no one's greater surprise than his own, he did just that! "Why," said Pooh, "just because Piglet can't have Halloween with us, there's no reason why we can't have Hallo*wasn't* with him!"

At Tigger's house, the fearless feline was putting the finishing touches on a ghost costume. Suddenly, Tigger's front door opened to reveal two figures covered in sheets.

"SPOOKABLES!" hollered Tigger, as he tried to

hide behind himself and tripped over his tail and fell.

The "spookables" removed their sheets, and Pooh and Eeyore grinned down at Tigger.

"We're on our way to Piglet's to have a Hallo*wasn't*," said Pooh. "Would you care to join us?"

"What are we standin' around here for?" Tigger said, snatching up his own ghost costume.

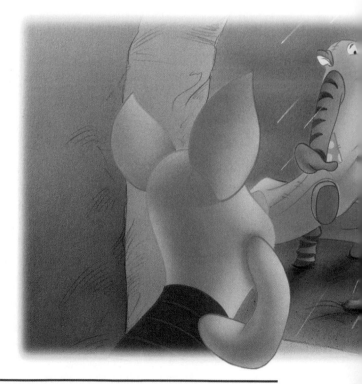

They had almost reached Piglet's house when a tree

branch snagged a corner of Pooh's bedsheet. Pooh was certain he'd been clutched by the cold claw of a spookable!

"Help!" shouted the startled Pooh. "Spookables!"

"Pooh Bear?" Piglet said. He had heard Pooh's shouts from inside his house.

Tigger and Eeyore, still wrapped in their ghostly bedsheets, were trying to free Pooh from the branch.

"Oh no!" Piglet cried. "Spookables have Pooh! I must save him, Halloween or no Halloween!"

Suddenly, Piglet noticed the spookable costume he had pulled together earlier.

"I'll show those spookables what tricking-and-treating is all about!" he cried, putting on the costume.

A few moments later, Piglet's

front door was thrown open. He walked outside, wearing the scary costume, determined to rescue Pooh.

"Boo?" said the spookable in a small voice. Then a bit louder, "Boo!"

Pooh, Eeyore, and Tigger looked up in horror and ran away down the path, leaving Pooh's costume in the possession of the tree branch.

They then ran past a startled Gopher, who was now clad in a Rabbit costume topped with long, floppy ears.

"Look out! Spookables!" they screamed.

Gopher-Rabbit looked up the path just as Piglet ran into him. They both went rolling after the others!

Rabbit, trying to keep his pumpkins dry with an umbrella, glanced up and had just enough time to mutter, "Oh no! Not again!" before Pooh, Tigger, and Eeyore collided into him.

Then, Piglet and Gopher collided into *them*, and
everyone went rolling as pieces of costume went flying.

Finally, they untangled themselves and discovered that there was not a single spookable to be seen.

"Help!" said Gopher. He was sitting in the middle of the garden, wearing a pumpkin!

"What a wonderful costume, Gopher," said a very impressed Eeyore.

"I particularly like your hat," agreed Rabbit.

"No doubt about it, Gopher," said Tigger, "it's the bestest costume yet!"

"Yippee!" Gopher cheered, stepping out of his costume and taking a bow. "I knew I could do it!"

"And I knew that Piglet could do it, too," said Pooh.

"Do what?" asked the puzzled Piglet.

"You saved us all," said Pooh. "You're here and the spookable isn't, so you must have chased it away."

"Say, that's right! Way to go, Piglet!" said Tigger.

All of Piglet's friends shook his very small hand as he puffed up with pride.

"Wait half a second, Piglet," said Tigger.

"You never did figure out what you're gonna be for Halloween."

"Oh but I have," Piglet said with a smile. "I've decided to go as Pooh's very best and very bravest friend!"

"And *that*," said Pooh, smiling down at Piglet, "is the thing I'd most like you to be."

WALT DISNEY'S

DONALD DUCK

AND THE WITCH NEXT DOOR

"Unca Donald, look!" called Huey Duck. "Someone built a house on the vacant lot next door!" cried Dewey Duck.

"I think we're going to have

a new neighbor," said Louie Duck.

Donald peeked over the fence. "By golly, you're right," he said. "But the house wasn't there yesterday. There was nothing on the lot last night. And what a funny-looking house! If I didn't know better, I'd say it was made out of gingerbread."

Dewey tasted a corner of the new house.

"It *is* made out of ginger-bread!" he said.

"A ginger-bread house!" cried Louie. "Only witches live in gingerbread houses. I read that in one of my storybooks."

"Witches?" Donald Duck said with a laugh. "There are no such things as witches."

At that moment, the door of the gingerbread house popped open. A lady with purple hair and big green eyes looked out. "Who doesn't believe in witches?" the lady cried out.

"I don't," said Donald.

"You will," she said. "My name is Madam Mim, and I built this house by magic."

"How?" asked Donald.

"Easy! I'm a witch!" She proved it by raising her hands and casting a spell.

POOF! Donald turned into a watermelon! Huey's, Dewey's, and Louie's eyes opened wide. They cried out, "We believe in witches! We believe! We do! Please, change that watermelon back into Unca Donald."

Madam Mim gave them a sly look. "I want some cobwebs for my new house. We witches like cobwebs— they make a place cozy, you know. I'll trade your uncle for some cobwebs."

"You bet!" the boys shouted, and they ran home to find some cobwebs.

Dewey gathered some in the garage and in the garden shed. Louie looked in the lumber pile. Huey searched

the cellar. They also swept some cobwebs from the chandelier, the attic, and the storeroom.

"Is that all?" asked Madam Mim when the boys brought her a basketful of cobwebs.

"It's all we have," Huey said.

"Then I suppose it will have to do," said Madam Mim. She changed the watermelon back into Donald Duck and went inside to decorate her new house with the cobwebs.

"What happened?" asked Donald, looking dazed. "I felt all green and cold!"

"Our new neighbor *is* a witch," said Huey. "She

turned you into a watermelon."

"Hmmmm," said Donald. "If she's a witch, I wonder if she has a flying broom."

Before another day had passed, they saw that Mim did indeed have a flying broom.

"Doesn't that look like fun?" Donald said happily. "I wonder if she'll let me borrow it now and then. After all, she *is* using our cobwebs."

"Don't ask, Unca Donald," said Louie. "She might change you back into a watermelon—or maybe a cabbage or even a rutabaga."

So, Donald Duck didn't ask Madam Mim if he could borrow her broomstick. Instead, he waited until she was busy planting toadstools in her backyard. Then he snatched the broom and flew away.

"Great, leaping bat wings!" shouted Madam Mim when she saw Donald on her broom.

Donald didn't know how to control the broom, and he was wobbling badly. But Mim knew all about brooms, and she was determined to teach Donald a lesson. She cast a spell, and the broom kicked like a wild mustang!

ZOOM! The broom flew up, up, up—right through a cloud.

"AHHH!" cried Donald Duck as he almost bumped into a passing eagle.

"Slow down! Slow down!" shouted Donald, but the broom went even faster. It sped across the sky. It raced with the starlings. It scattered the blue-birds, and it broke up a formation of migrating geese.

"Easy! Easy!" Donald said pleadingly, but the broom didn't take it easy. It crashed through a high-flying kite. It played tag with a jetliner. It bucked and swerved and looped. It zigged and zagged and rolled— and it tossed Donald off.

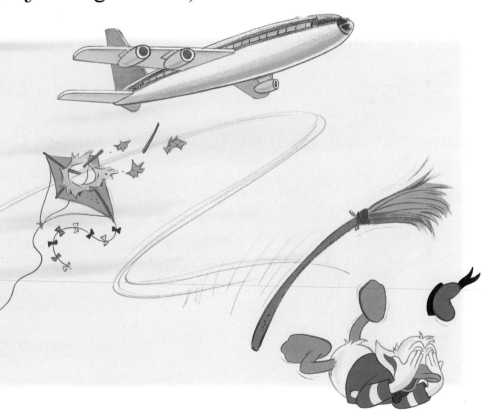

Donald fell down, down, down until . . . *BUMP!*
He landed on a damp, soggy island in the middle of
Great Dismal Swamp. And who should be waiting on
that damp, soggy island—but Madam Mim, of course!

The broom fell to the ground and leaned against Madam Mim. "My poor broom!" she said. "It's so tired, it can hardly stand up. I'll teach you a lesson, you thieving duck!" And she changed Donald into a frog.

"There!" she said. "For all I care, you can stay here in the swamp forever." Then she got on her broom and flew home.

Donald didn't stay in the swamp forever. Madam

Mim had forgotten that frogs can hop and swim.

Donald hopped and swam, and swam and hopped, until

he was safe on dry ground.

"I'll never steal a broom again," said Donald to himself. "I'll never take anything!" Suddenly, Donald wasn't a frog anymore. He was Donald Duck. He hurried home as fast as his webbed feet could carry him.

"Drat!" said Madam Mim when she saw Donald walking by. "He's back. Well, if he's going to live here, I'm not! But before I go, I'll give him back his cobwebs—with some interest!"

So, Madam Mim called all her friends together. They came from far and near and brought hundreds and hundreds of cobwebs— and even a few spiders.

"What a

mess!" yelled

Donald. After

he settled down,

he said to the

boys, "Bring me

a broom."

"Our broom

doesn't fly," said Huey.

"Thank goodness!" said Donald, and he began to

sweep up the cobwebs and spiders.

The boys didn't stay to watch. They knew just what to do when a neighbor moves away and leaves a gingerbread house behind. They hurried over and ate the gingerbread house—right down to the very last gingerbread shingle!

Who's That Ghost?

It was a dark, rainy day. Jasmine stared out the window. "I'm so bored. I wish we could take a walk outside," she said with a sigh.

"Don't let the bad weather get you down," Aladdin said. "We can still go for a walk!"

"But there's a storm outside," said Jasmine.

"We can walk through the palace," said Aladdin as he reached for Jasmine's hand.

Meanwhile, the Genie was also feeling bored. But

when he overheard Aladdin and Jasmine's plan, he got a brilliant idea.

"I think it's time for a little rainy-day fun!" he said with a laugh.

Aladdin and Jasmine began walking through the palace. Outside, the wind howled. Jasmine jumped as thunder boomed and lightning flashed. Abu, their pet monkey, came running from

the other room and hopped right on Aladdin's shoulder.

"It's just a little storm," Aladdin said calmly. "We're safe inside the palace."

Aladdin led Jasmine through a shortcut. "This will take us to the kitchen. So, when we're done with our walk, we can have a royal snack!" Aladdin said.

"I already know where the kitchen is," said Jasmine.

"But this is a super shortcut. You'll see," said Aladdin. What Aladdin

didn't know was that he had taken a wrong turn and was heading toward a very different place. . . .

As they continued walking, the air began to feel cold. *"Ahhhhhh!"* Abu screeched as he walked right into a cobweb. He

chattered and jumped onto Aladdin's shoulder for safety.

"Are you sure this is the way to the kitchen?" Jasmine asked nervously.

Aladdin nodded. But he wasn't sure at all.

"It's just a little farther," Aladdin said. But he didn't recall the shortcut being quite so cold and damp—or so dark.

Just then, he saw a door up ahead. "Aha!" he said, relieved. "That must be the door that leads to the kitchen!"

Slowly, he opened the door. Suddenly, hundreds of squealing bats flew out at them and circled over their heads. Jasmine screamed. Abu closed his eyes tightly and chattered. "Let's get out of here!" yelled Aladdin.

And they all began to run.

They ran as fast as they could down a long
hallway. At the end of the hallway stood a door. "In
here!" shouted Aladdin as they ran for cover. Once
they had slammed the door shut, the three of them
huddled together, trying to catch their breath.

"Whew!" said Aladdin. "Glad that's over. I think this was the door we were supposed to go through in the first place."

Jasmine and Abu followed as Aladdin led the way.

"Uh . . . just a few more steps and we'll be making ice-cream sundaes," Aladdin said.

But a few more steps led them into one of the darkest, coldest, and spookiest places they had ever been—the dungeon.

They all looked around nervously. Just then, the sound of laughter surrounded them. Abu's teeth started to chatter. Jasmine felt a shiver run down her spine.

A voice boomed, "Even if you scream and shout, I don't think I'll let you out!"

"Who are you?" asked Aladdin. "Show yourself."

"Here I am—your lovely host. I'm the creepy dungeon ghost!" shouted the ghost as he appeared in front of them.

They couldn't believe their eyes. They had all heard about the ghosts that lived in the dungeon, but they had never dreamed they'd meet one.

Then, just as quickly as it had appeared, the ghost disappeared.

"Don't worry, Jasmine. I'll get you out of here safely," Aladdin assured her.

Then, Aladdin led Jasmine and Abu in another direction. He was desperately searching for a door or secret exit. A cold wind blew through the air.

They walked quickly through the twisting halls of the dungeon. It was eerie and quiet.

Just then, the floor gave way. All three of them went flying down a chute.

"Aaaaahhhhh!" shouted Aladdin, Jasmine, and Abu. They landed with a thump.

Suddenly, the ghost appeared again. "Nice trip?" he said with a laugh.

Aladdin and Jasmine looked at each other.

This ghost was starting to remind them of someone they knew. They decided to try to find out who the ghost was. "Hey, do we know you?" asked Aladdin.

"I'll say!" said the ghost, chuckling.

Jasmine turned to Aladdin
and raised her eyebrows.
Aladdin looked closely
at the ghost. There was
something *very* familiar
about this ghost. The
two walked closer to it.

"And do you know
who I am?" asked Jasmine.

"Yeah, you're Princess Jasmine—Al's girl!"
answered the ghost.

"Aha!" shouted Aladdin. "Got ya!"

"You're not a ghost. You're the Genie," Jasmine said.

"Oops, caught me!" said the Genie, turning back into himself. "I lose!"

"That wasn't very funny, Genie," said Aladdin.

"Yeah, you really scared us," said Jasmine.

Abu chattered angrily.

"I'm sorry," said the Genie. "But you did say you were bored. It was just a little rainy-day fun."

Jasmine and Aladdin couldn't help laughing.

"Now, can you get us out of here?" asked Aladdin.

"Yes, sir," said the Genie as he quickly turned into a giant flashlight and began to lead them to the kitchen.

Soon, they were eating ice-cream sundaes.

"I guess I did a pretty good job of scaring up some ice cream," said the Genie.

Everyone laughed. A boring rainy day with the Genie around? Never!

Disney's

TARZAN ®

ONE BRAVE GORILLA

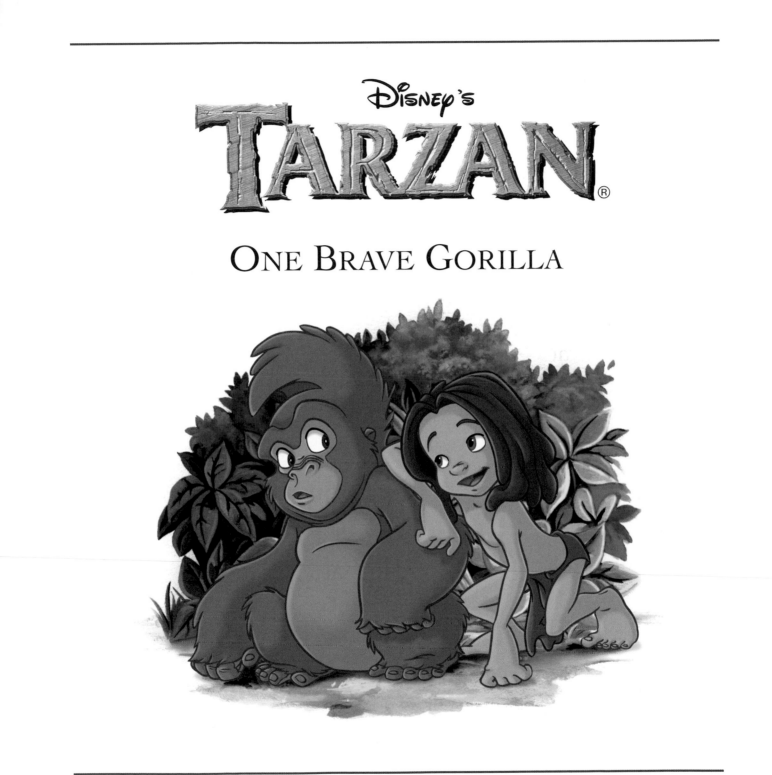

"Hey, Terk! Wait up!" Tarzan cried as he raced through the jungle.

Terk rolled her eyes. "Oh, great," she murmured to her friends Flynt and Mungo. "Tarzan is following us again."

"What should we do?" Mungo asked.

"We can't let him come

to the waterfall with us," Flynt said. "You remember what happened the last time."

"I remember," Terk said, shaking her head as she recalled the elephant stampede Tarzan had caused.

"What are you guys doing?" Tarzan asked as he hurried over to them.

"We're just going for a walk," Terk said quickly, faking a yawn. "Just a boring old walk in the boring old jungle."

"A walk?" Tarzan asked. "Sounds fun! Can I come?"

Terk looked at Flynt and Mungo, who shook their heads. Oh, man, thought Terk. I hate it when Tarzan does that. Maybe I can talk him out of coming. . . .

"Hmm," Terk said. "I'm not sure that you'd really want to join us. The part of the jungle that we're going to is kind of scary."

"Scary?" Tarzan repeated. "What do you mean?"

"Well, we'll be close to where the horrible slithernix lives," Terk said, crossing her fingers behind her back.

"What's a slithernix?" Tarzan asked.

"It's a horrible, hideous monster," Terk said, "with sharp, slobbery teeth and steely claws!"

"A slithernix doesn't scare me," Tarzan said. "I can fight it off."

"Yeah, well," Terk said, "if you're not afraid of the slithernix, maybe you'll be afraid of the gobbling quicksand. It'll swallow you whole!"

"I can use a vine to swing over the quicksand," Tarzan said.

"Oh, no," Terk said. "You can't use a vine. There are slippery, slithery snakes in the trees that will attack you."

"I'm not afraid of snakes," Tarzan said. "I've seen plenty."

"But these snakes are poisonous," Terk said.

"Gee, Terk," Flynt whispered, "I don't like the sound of those snakes."

"Yeah," Mungo agreed. "And I don't like the sound of that slithernix, either!"

Terk rolled her eyes. Of course, there were no snakes near the waterfall. Or quicksand. And there was no such thing as a slithernix. She had just wanted to scare Tarzan so he would stay behind.

But, so far, the only ones who were frightened by Terk's stories were Flynt and Mungo!

"Okay, Tarzan," Terk said finally. "You can come."

"Hooray!" Tarzan cried. He jumped up happily and grabbed onto a nearby vine. But the vine broke, and he fell face first onto the ground.

"Just try to stay out of trouble," Terk said with a sigh. She waited for Tarzan to pick himself up and then quickly walked deeper into the jungle.

Flynt and Mungo were right behind her.

"Hey, Terk," Mungo whispered, "why did you let Tarzan come with us?"

"Yeah," Flynt said. "What's the big idea?"

"Just keep moving," Terk said. "If Tarzan can't keep up, maybe he'll give up and go home."

"Good thinking," Mungo whispered.

Terk nodded. She hated it when Tarzan looked sad, but she also knew that if he came to the waterfall, it would be a disaster!

Sure enough, after a while, Terk, Mungo, and Flynt couldn't see Tarzan behind them anymore. And a little while after that, they couldn't hear him, either.

"See?" Terk grinned. "Tarzan has gone home already."

By now, the gorillas had walked deep into the jungle. It was dark. And very creepy.

"Are you sure that this is the right way to the waterfall?" Mungo asked.

"I *think* it is," Terk said. She stopped and looked around, and realized that she wasn't really sure. Terk had taken a winding path through the jungle so that

Tarzan would have trouble following them. And now it looked as if they were lost.

Just then, there was a loud squawk. Terk jumped!

"What was that?"
Mungo asked.

"Just a bird," Terk
said. "I think."

"I don't mind birds,"
Flynt said. "I just
hope we don't run
into any of those snakes!"

"Or the slithernix!" Mungo agreed.

"Oh, there's no such thing as a slithernix," Terk said,
her voice wavering.

But Terk began thinking of sharp teeth and steely claws. What if there really *was* a slithernix?

Suddenly, the bushes started rustling!

"Yikes!" Mungo cried as he jumped back and knocked Flynt over.

They both fell backward into a large mud puddle. "The quicksand!" Flynt shouted. "It's gonna get us!"

"I'll save you!" Terk cried. She ran to her friends and grabbed Flynt's arm. But it was covered in mud. As Terk tried to drag them out, her hand slipped, and she stumbled backward against a tree. A bunch of vines fell around her.

"Snakes!" Terk shrieked. "They're everywhere! Somebody help me!"

"Terk! Are you okay?" someone shouted. Just then, a small figure jumped out of the bushes and began tugging at the vines that were all around Terk.

It took Terk a moment to realize that she was covered in vines—not snakes. And the figure helping her was Tarzan!

"Tarzan, what are you doing here?" Terk cried.

"What do you mean?" Tarzan asked. "Remember? I'm going with you guys to the waterfall!"

He walked over to Flynt and Mungo and helped them out of the mud.
"And it looks as if you could use a waterfall right now!" Tarzan said with a grin.

"You're one brave gorilla," said Terk.

Flynt and Mungo looked at each other,

embarrassed. Tarzan *had* been brave—braver

than they had been!

"So, what are we waiting for?" Tarzan

asked. "Let's go to the waterfall!"

And so they did. And there wasn't a

slithernix in sight!

Peter Pan

CAPTAIN HOOK'S SHADOW

"Walk the plank, you blasted Peter Pan!" John cried as he waved his wooden sword at Michael. John was pretending to be evil Captain Hook, and Michael was pretending to be Peter Pan.

"I *won't* walk the plank," Michael said, "and you're a codfish, Captain Hook!"

"I'll get you

for that, Peter Pan!" John cried, imitating Captain
Hook's sneer.

Michael leaped off the bed, wooden sword drawn.
Clack! Clack! The brothers chased each other around the
nursery in a sword fight. For a moment, Michael felt
just as he had when he was a Lost Boy in Never Land.

"All right, John and Michael, time for bed," Wendy said, as she walked into the nursery.

"Just a few more minutes," Michael begged. "Captain Hook is about to make me walk the plank!"

"You'll have plenty of time to walk the plank tomorrow," Wendy said. "Now it's time to sleep."

Groaning, Michael and John put down their swords and crawled into their beds as Wendy turned out the light.

Michael pulled the covers up to his chin, and found the cool spot on his pillow. He was comfortable, but he wasn't tired at all.

Soon, Michael could tell by the gentle breathing in the next bed that John was already asleep. Michael squeezed his eyes shut, but it was no use. He kept picturing evil Captain Hook trying to capture Peter Pan—and the surprised look on the pirate's face when Peter got away!

Suddenly, there was a rattling sound, then a *whoosh.*

Michael opened his eyes and saw that the nursery windows were wide open. Had someone gotten inside?

That's when Michael noticed a shadow against the far wall. He gasped. The shadow was shaped just like Captain Hook! Could it be?

Quickly, Michael dove under the covers, shaking. But being under the covers didn't make him feel any better. If Captain Hook was in the nursery, Michael decided, then he wanted to know for certain.

Slowly, Michael lifted the bottom edge of his blanket and peeked out.

Michael still couldn't see Hook, but the captain's shadow was right there against the wall—large as life. The shadow looked around the nursery for a moment, then caught sight of something. On tiptoe, it began to creep toward the far corner.

A chill ran down Michael's spine.

Captain Hook was heading toward Wendy!

Michael knew he had to do something—he couldn't let Captain Hook take her. He glanced around the nursery, and his eye fell on something lying beside his bed, right beneath his hand. It was his wooden sword!

Michael reached down and wrapped his fingers around the sword just as the shadow got to Wendy.

Quickly, Michael threw off his covers and leaped toward the shadow!

The shadow stumbled backward. Michael lunged at it again, but it swiped at him with its hook!

Quickly, Michael dove under his bed. The shadow reached for him, but Michael scooted away just in time!

Then the shadow leaped onto the bed, and Michael gulped, waiting for the sharp hook to swipe at him again. He began to wonder why he was only seeing Captain Hook's shadow and not Hook himself.

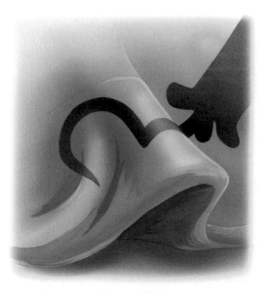

But there was no time to think about that now. Michael realized he couldn't stay under the bed—Captain Hook was sure to get to him sooner or later!

Michael darted out from under the bed, but the shadow jumped after him. Gasping, Michael stumbled backward and tripped over a ball lying on the floor.

The shadow skulked toward him slowly. Now Captain Hook has got me for sure, Michael thought. Shivering, he pictured the Crocodile that waited for anyone who walked the plank.

"Cock-a-doodle-doo!" a voice cried suddenly.

"Peter Pan!" Michael shouted, as his hero flew in through the window.

"There it is!" Peter cried. "It's Captain Hook's shadow! Don't let it get away!" The shadow tried to run, but Peter flew after it.

"What?" Michael said. "It's only a shadow?"

Michael picked himself up off the floor and ran after

the shadow, too.

The shadow leaped

onto the wooden

toy chest.

"Grab it from the

other side!"

Peter called.

Michael ran toward

the shadow from the right as Peter flew at it from the

left. The shadow was now trapped!

In a flash, Michael reached out and caught the shadow.

"Put it in here!" Peter cried, holding out a sack.

Michael stuffed the shadow into the sack, and Peter tied it closed with a piece of rope.

"Whew!" Peter said. "That was close."

"What was Captain Hook's shadow doing here?" Michael asked.

"I stole the shadow for a prank," Peter explained. "Some prank! That shadow  has been nothing but trouble—pulling the Lost Boys' tails and putting pinecones in their beds. And then it sneaked away from Never Land."

"How awful!" Michael cried.

Peter nodded. "I have to fly back to Never Land and return it right away, while everyone aboard Captain Hook's ship is still asleep."

"Good idea," Michael said.

"Do you want to come with me?" Peter asked. "It'll be a great adventure!"

"I don't think I'd want to go without Wendy and John," Michael said.

"Then, let's bring them!" Peter said as he flew over to Wendy's bed. He reached down to give her a gentle shake, but then drew his hand back.

"Aw, she's fast asleep," he said.

Peter looked over at John and said, "John's fast asleep, too."

"Maybe next time," Michael said.

"Next time," Peter echoed, jumping to the window ledge. "Good-bye, Michael. Tell Wendy and John I said hello!" he called as he flew off into the night.

"I will!" Michael promised. He sat in the window seat, smiling — glad to have had his very own real-life adventure with Peter Pan.

The Sunken Ship

I t was a bright, warm summer morning. The sun's rays shone down, sending shafts of light deep into the waters of the ocean.

Under the sea, Ariel, the Little Mermaid, stretched in her giant clamshell bed.

"What a perfect day for exploring," she said to her friend Flounder.

Ariel loved to explore the dark caves and brightly colored coral reefs in the ocean. She had found some wonderful things there. But most of Ariel's true treasures came from sunken ships. The ships were filled with trinkets from the human world—a world that Ariel longed to be a part of.

"Ariel!" called Flounder, flapping his fins as fast as he could. "Wait for me!"

Ariel glanced back at her friend. "Come on, slow-poke," she said, teasing him. "We have to find more shells for Alana's present." Ariel was making a special gift for her sister's birthday—a beautiful shell necklace.

Just then, Ariel spotted a row of glittering shells. She picked them up, one by one, until she stopped right at the mouth of a sunken ship!

"Wow!" said Ariel. "Let's go inside. Maybe we'll find lots of treasures."

"Or we could just look *outside*," Flounder offered. He was afraid of sunken ships.

But it was too late. Ariel had already disappeared inside. Flounder hurried to catch up with her.

The ship was dark and eerily silent.

"There's s-s-something s-s-spooky about this ship," Flounder stuttered.

"Oh, don't be such a guppy," Ariel said with a laugh. "I just know I'm going to find something special today."

Ariel and Flounder passed by a broken window. It cast a dark shadow over them. Suddenly, they heard the most terrifying sound. *RUFFF! RUFFF! RUFFF!* The noise was coming from somewhere inside the ship!

"I think it might be a monster!" cried Ariel, dropping her bag of shells.

"Let's g-g-get out of here!" cried Flounder.

For once, Ariel wasn't about to argue. She grabbed Flounder, and they started to make their way out.

Just as they reached the entrance of the ship, they swam right into Sebastian the crab.

"Ahhhh!" Ariel and Flounder both screamed. They hadn't expected to see Sebastian. But he had followed them to the ship. Ariel's father, King Triton, had ordered Sebastian to keep an eye on his daughter. And that's exactly what he was doing.

Ariel began to tell Sebastian about the noise that she had heard.

"Don't be silly, Ariel," Sebastian said. "You're making a big deal out of nothing again."

Suddenly, they heard the noise once more. *RUFFF! RUFFF! RUFFF!*

"Something is definitely in there!" Sebastian cried. "And it doesn't sound too happy! Let's get out of here!"

That night, Ariel couldn't stop thinking about the scary noise coming from the spooky ship. She climbed into bed and fell into a restless sleep. She dreamed she

was back in the ship with Flounder. They were being chased by a hideous monster. It had webbed feet, sunken yellow eyes, and long, razor-sharp teeth.

"Help!" cried Ariel.

"Help!" yelled Flounder.

"RUFFF! RUFFF! RUFFF!" cried the monster. Suddenly, the monster reached out and grabbed Flounder. The monster swallowed  him in one gulp. Next, he reached for Ariel.

"No!" screamed Ariel. "Leave me alone!"

"Ariel, wake up!" called King Triton.

Ariel sat up and rubbed her eyes.

"It is the middle of the night, daughter," explained the king. "You were having a nightmare."

Ariel told her father about her spooky dream and the terrifying monster.

"Only humans believe in monsters," King Triton said, trying to comfort her.

The next morning, Ariel gave Flounder a giant hug.

"What was that for?" asked the little fish.

"You were eaten by a horrible monster in my dream last night," Ariel said.

Flounder's eyes grew large. Then, they grew even larger when Ariel told him what she had planned for the day.

"We're going back to that ship," said Ariel, dragging Flounder along. "I left my bag of beautiful shells in there."

"I think I'll w-w-wait out here," said Flounder, once they arrived at the ship.

Ariel's heart pounded as she slipped inside.

It was very dark but Ariel soon spotted her bag.
Then, just as she was turning to leave, she heard the
terrifying sound. *RUFFF! RUFFF! RUFFF!*

At that moment, Ariel made a decision. Monster or
no monster, she just had to find out what was making
that noise!

Deeper and deeper Ariel plunged into the long narrow ship. The noise grew louder and louder. Ariel tried not to think of the monster with the razor-sharp teeth from her dream. She closed her eyes. But when she opened them, the noisy monster was standing right in front of her! Only the monster wasn't really a monster at all. It was a smiling toy dog.

He was made of metal, with a leash and a collar that read ROVER on it. He didn't look scary at all, thought Ariel.

"Aren't you the cutest thing," said Ariel, laughing. She carried it outside to where Flounder was waiting.

"I'll bet Scuttle will know what this human thing is called," said Ariel.

Scuttle was a seagull who claimed to know everything about the world of humans. Ariel and Flounder brought it to him.

"Ah, yes," said Scuttle. "This is a windup toy dog called a 'woofnhoofer.' Little humans are very fond of these.

"In fact," continued Scuttle, "I think I know the little one who lost this toy dog. She was crying on the beach the other day. It seems the toy dog got swept away by the waves. It must have ended up in the sunken ship."

Ariel frowned. "Then we must return it to her," she said.

And so, Scuttle dropped the toy dog on the beach near a little girl who was busy collecting shells.

"Rover!" cried the little girl, hugging the dog to her chest. She twirled around in a circle, smiling at the toy.

Ariel's heart melted as she watched the happy reunion. She would never forget her adventure in the spooky ship and the special treasure she had discovered.

And now, Ariel headed home so she could finally finish the necklace for her sister's birthday.

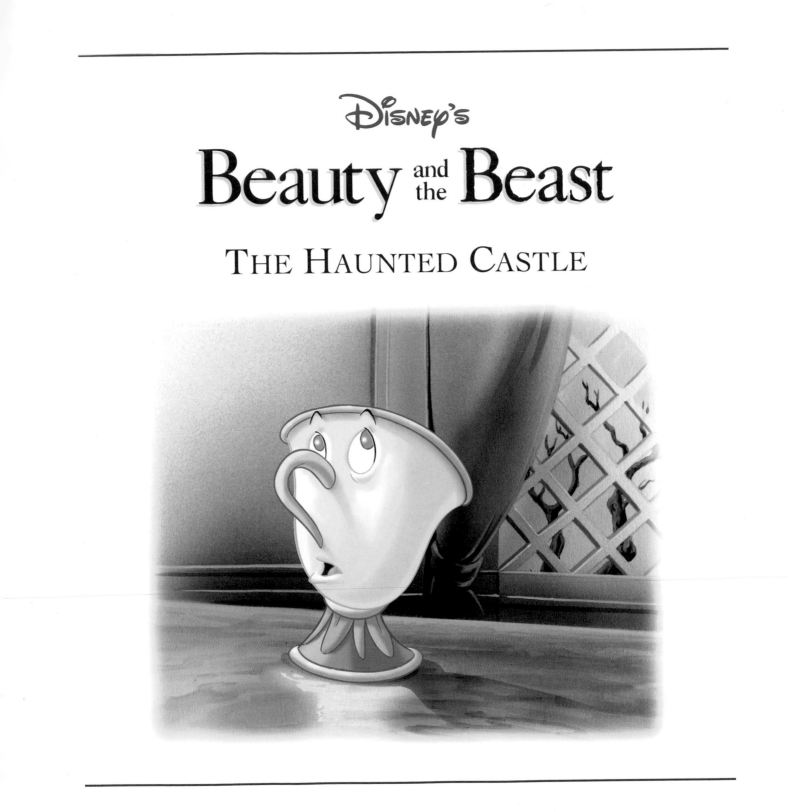

Disney's Beauty and the Beast

THE HAUNTED CASTLE

"Oh, Mama!" Chip wailed as his mother, Mrs. Potts, ran the water in the sink. "Why do I have to take a bath?"

"Now, now, Chip," Mrs. Potts said as she gave Chip a good scrubbing with a sponge. "You want to look your best for your birthday tomorrow, don't you?"

"I guess so." Chip giggled. "That tickles," he said as Mrs. Potts patted him dry with a towel.

"All right, we're all done," Mrs. Potts said.

"Look, Belle!" Chip cried as Belle walked into the kitchen. "I'm clean as a whistle!"

Belle laughed. "You look very nice," she said. "Are you excited about your birthday tomorrow?"

"Am I!" Chip cried happily. "Mama says that we'll play lots of games. Isn't that right, Mama?"

Mrs. Potts nodded. "That's right, Chip," she said.

"Do you think I'll have a birthday cake, too?" Chip asked Belle.

"Well, I don't know," Belle said, winking at Mrs. Potts. "I guess you'll just have to wait and see."

Just then, Chip yawned.

"All right, Chip, time for bed," Mrs. Potts said as she nudged him toward the china cabinet.

"But how can I sleep when I'm so excited about my birthday?" Chip asked, yawning again.

"Oh, I think you'll manage," Mrs. Potts said as she gave him a quick kiss. "Good night."

"Good night, Chip," Belle said.

"Good night," Chip said. His eyelids were very droopy. In another minute, he was fast asleep.

A few hours later, Chip woke up with a start. The kitchen was very dark. There wasn't even a crack of light coming in from the door to the hallway. Everyone must be asleep, Chip thought. He blinked sleepily.

Suddenly, he heard a long, slow creak, and then the rattle of metal. It must be coming from the silverware drawer, thought Chip.

"Who's there?" Chip whispered into the darkness. But nobody answered.

Then the noise stopped. But soon it started again, more quickly this time.

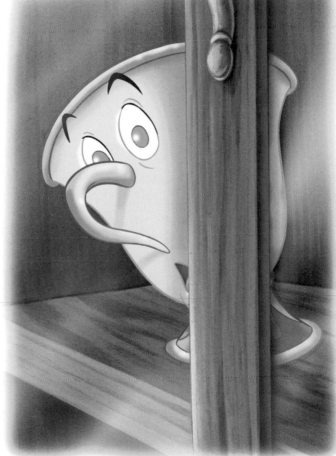

Chip shivered. "Come out and show yourself!" he said, trying to be brave. He wished that there were some light in the kitchen. He couldn't see a thing.

Suddenly, the drawer closed with a bang. Then, Chip heard footsteps, and the low click of the door closing.

"I better go see who it is," Chip said as he jumped out of the china cabinet. "What if it's a ghost—or a monster. I'll go warn Mama and Belle, and they'll wake the Beast." Chip was pretty sure the Beast could scare away any ghost or monster that got into the castle . . .

as long as someone

warned

him

in time.

Carefully, Chip climbed down from the table and hopped into the hall. Someone had forgotten to close the curtains, and the light of the moon shone into the hallway. But Chip still couldn't see very well. Suddenly, a floorboard squeaked! Chip ducked behind some draperies.

Then Chip heard voices.

"I've got them," a voice whispered.

"Good. Let's go," another voice said. "The others are waiting."

Others? Chip thought. Could the house be *full* of ghosts and monsters? Chip was scared.

Sure enough, the floorboards above Chip's head let out a low squeak. The ghosts and monsters were everywhere!

Thud, thud, thud. The creatures were making their way up the stairs. Chip peeked out from behind the curtains to see what they looked like.

But it was still too dark — Chip couldn't see very well. If Chip wanted to get a better look at the creatures, then he was going to have to follow them up the stairs.

The little teacup hopped up the stairs quietly. When

he reached the second floor, he stopped.

Along the wall, Chip saw a long shadow. It must be one of the monsters, he thought. It was enormous and had a large bumpy head and sharp claws. It was even more frightening than the Beast!

Finally,

the shadow of the monster disappeared into a room.

Chip just *had* to see what the monsters looked like, so he decided to go in. He took a deep breath and quickly hopped to the door and let it swing open. When he saw what was inside, he let out a gasp!

"Chip!" Belle cried. "What are you doing up so late?"

"My heavens!" Cogsworth, the mantel clock, shouted as he dropped the large present he was carrying. "We haven't even finished decorating for your surprise breakfast birthday party yet!"

"Surprise party?" Chip asked. "You mean there are no ghosts or monsters?"

"Goodness, no," said Lumiere, the candelabrum.

"Why were you in the kitchen?" Chip asked.

Cogsworth held up a pair of scissors. "We needed these from the silverware drawer," he explained. "To cut the streamers."

Belle laughed. "Well," she said, "I guess this really *was* a surprise!"

Chip grinned. He was glad that the surprise had

turned out to be a party, and not a bunch of ghosts and monsters!

"Thanks, everyone," he said happily. "This is the best birthday surprise ever!"

WHERE'S WOODY?

It was a typical Sunday afternoon at Andy's house, or so everyone thought.

Andy was downstairs, watching a movie with his mom, and the toys were playing kickball in his room.

"Yee-hah!" cowgirl Jessie yelled as she kicked the ball and raced toward the book they were using as first base.

Buzz Lightyear

ran from first base to second.

"I got it!" Hamm cried, chasing the Ping-Pong

ball. "Uh-oh! I . . . I don't got it." The ball sailed over his head.

Woody leaped toward the ball. The cowboy was playing outfield from his place on top of the desk.

"I got it!" Woody exclaimed as he caught the ball.
But Woody didn't see the roller skate on the windowsill.
"Whoa!" he cried as he fell onto the skate and went
rolling right out of Andy's bedroom window!

"Oh, my gosh!"
Jessie shouted as
she scrambled up
the desk and ran
to the window.
"Woody! Are you
all right?"

"I'm fine," Woody yelled from the backyard. "But would oh—hey! Stop that! Stop! Oh, no! Look out!"

"I can't see Woody," Jessie said. "Woody, where are you?" she called. But there was no reply.

"It sounds like Woody's in trouble!" Buzz said.

"We have to save him!" Jessie cried.

The toys tried to lower Buzz into the backyard on a yo-yo. But he rolled right back up again.

Jessie suggested they try Slinky Dog. So, Slinky used his spring and lowered Jessie and Buzz to the ground.

The back-yard was very big and very scary. And there was still no sign of Woody.

"Where could he be?" Jessie asked.

A strange, hooting noise came from above.

"What was that?" Buzz asked. He was ready to tackle anything that came near them.

"I think it's just a hoot owl," Jessie said. "They're harmless."

"Harmless, eh?" Buzz said doubtfully. He peered around, still on his guard.

A rustling noise came from the tree.

"What was that?" Buzz asked again.

Jessie gulped. "Probably just a squirrel," she said.

Buzz frowned up at the tree.

"Where should we start looking?" Jessie whispered. She turned to face Buzz, just in time to see an enormous bird swooping down toward him! "Duck!" she shouted.

Instead of ducking, Buzz looked behind him. "That's not a duck," he cried, "it's an owl—whoa!"

The owl grabbed Buzz and began to fly away.

"Buzz—wait for me!" Jessie yelled as she ran after the bird. Jessie had to save Buzz, so she took a running leap and grabbed Buzz's leg. The owl flew toward a big tree in Andy's neighbor's backyard. "Yikes!" Jessie cried as they soared through the air, high above the ground.

Finally, the owl set Jessie and Buzz down

on a tree branch, and pecked at Buzz with its sharp

beak.

"Hey!" Buzz said. "Stop that.
If I weren't made of plastic,
that would really hurt!"

The bird pecked
at him again.

"I believe this
bird thinks we're
dinner," Jessie
said nervously.

"I thought you said owls were harmless," Buzz said.

"Maybe that's sparrows," Jessie admitted. "I'm a toy, not a bird expert!"

"All right, stand back and let me handle this," Buzz said. He turned to the owl. "Excuse me. We are looking for our friend, Woody."

"Whoo?" the owl asked.

"Woody," Buzz said. "He's a cowboy, kind of tall, wears a gold star."

"Whoo—whoo—whoo?" the owl asked.

"Wood-y," Buzz repeated slowly. "If you would just —"

The owl pecked at Buzz again. This time Buzz went tumbling off the tree branch!

"Buzz!" Jessie cried. "Are you okay?"

The owl looked at Jessie. "Whoo?" it said.

"Go away!" Jessie warned, but the bird hopped toward her on its sharp claws. Jessie was scared. She wasn't plastic like Buzz, and the owl could hurt her. Jessie looked down and saw a large birdbath.

"Geronimo!" she cried as she jumped from the tree.

Splash!

"Buzz!" Jessie shouted from the birdbath.

"Down here!" Buzz called, climbing out of the sandbox he had fallen into. "I'm okay. No sign of Woody, though."

Jessie swallowed hard. Overhead, the wind howled through the tree branches. Jessie shivered as she thought of the owl's large eyes peering down at them.

Suddenly, they heard a voice. "Want to go out, Mr. Whiskers?" the voice asked. Andy's neighbor's back door opened, and a big cat strutted into the yard.

When Mr. Whiskers saw Buzz, he crouched, ready to spring.

Jessie gasped. A cat could carry off a toy and leave it far from home. "Don't move," she said to Buzz.

The cat stared at her. Jessie bit her lip in fear.

What if Mr. Whiskers had already gotten Woody?

What if he got them, too?

Just then, a ball rolled into the yard.

"Go get it, Buster!" Woody's voice shouted.

The cat turned as Andy's dog ran into the yard.

Buster barked, and Mr. Whiskers let out a hiss and ran into the house through the cat door.

"Good dog!" Buzz said as Jessie climbed down from the birdbath.

"Buzz! Jessie!" Woody shouted as he ran up to them. "What are you guys doing out here?"

"We heard you calling for help," Jessie explained.

"Oh, that," Woody said, looking embarrassed. "Buster jumped on me and knocked me down. I thought you knew I was okay. I didn't mean to make you worry."

"We're glad you're all right," Buzz said.

All three toys climbed onto Buster's back. He carried them back to Andy's house and inside through the dog door.

"Thanks for

worrying about me," Woody said, once they were safely back in Andy's room.

"Anytime, Woody," Jessie said. Jessie was glad that she and Buzz were able to find Woody, even though the backyard had been kind of scary.

Buzz nodded. "That's what friends are for," he said.

MONSTERS, INC.

THE SPOOKY SLUMBER PARTY

It was a quiet morning at Monsters, Inc. The new president, James P. Sullivan (also known as Sulley), had gotten in early to catch up on his paperwork. Sulley smiled as he reviewed the monthly laugh reports. A few months earlier, the company had gone through a big change. Instead of using screams, they now converted children's laughs into energy. It made everyone—monsters and kids alike—a lot happier.

Suddenly, the phone rang. "Hello?" said Sulley.

"It's Dispatch," said the voice at the other end of the line. "Annual slumber party at little Shannon Brown's house. Waxford is out sick. We need a replacement."

"I'll get right on it," said Sulley.

Lots of kids means lots of laughs, thought Sulley. He

wanted to make sure he had his best monster on the

case. Sulley didn't have to

think about it for long.

What better monster for the

job than his one-eyed pal,

Mike Wazowski? Mike was

the top laugh collector at

Monsters, Inc., and Sulley

knew his best friend would

be perfect for the job.

Mike was in
the locker room,
getting ready for
work. He had just
finished putting in
his contact lens—

which was the size of a pizza—when Sulley walked in.

Sulley explained the situation to Mike.

"I'm your man," said Mike.

"Great!" said Sulley. Whistling, he went back to his

office to finish his laugh reports.

"Piece of cake," Mike said as a door slid into his station. "One joke, and I'll collect enough energy for the year!" Then Mike burst through the closet door. But oddly enough, the room was empty.

"Uh . . . hello?" said Mike. He looked around the room, but there was no slumber party in sight. Mike peeked under the bed—but there was nothing there, either. Hmm . . . I wonder where everyone is, he thought. Maybe I should just head back.

Just as Mike started walking back toward the closet, he heard the faint sound of laughter.

"All right, now we are in business," Mike said out loud. "Kids, prepare to laugh."

But just then, thunder cracked across the sky. And lightning flashed through the room. Mike jumped. If

there was one thing Mike didn't like, it was a thunderstorm.

"I'm okay! I'm fine!" Mike shouted. Then he ran to the closet door to return to the factory.

But there was no way out. Mike kept trying the door, but it wasn't leading back to Monsters, Inc. It just opened into the closet. Mike soon realized that lightning must have struck the door, causing it to malfunction.

"Don't panic, don't panic," Mike repeated, his voice shaking. He knew he had to find the slumber party and another closet door—fast.

Mike took a deep breath, rubbed his eye, and headed out of the room and into the dark hallway. He was sure he heard laughter coming from somewhere. Now all he had to do was find it.

As he started walking, the floor creaked beneath

him. Halfway down the dark hallway, Mike stopped and looked around. There were paintings on the wall that looked very creepy and gave him goose bumps. He was pretty sure the people in the paintings were staring right at him. "I gotta get out of here," Mike muttered to himself as he continued down the hallway. But he suddenly stopped in his tracks.

Mike couldn't believe his eye. At the end of the hall was a large furry creature—with fangs. It was panting heavily.

As Mike walked toward the creature, it lunged at him, knocking him down. Within seconds, it began to lick Mike. "Ahhhhhh!" he shouted. "Dog breath!" Mike hated dogs!

He pushed the dog away and ran into a nearby room. He slammed the door shut.

Meanwhile, back at Monsters, Inc., Sulley was working down on the Laugh Floor when the floor manager came running over. He reported that Mike still hadn't returned from the slumber party. When Sulley went to check on the door, he discovered it had malfunctioned.

"Uh-oh," said Sulley. "I gotta help my little buddy."

So, Sulley brought in a maintenance crew to fix the door.

Together, the monsters pulled
levers and pushed buttons. They
even read from the emergency
Monsters, Inc., manuals. Sulley

and the monsters

worked long and hard to figure out

how to get

the door to

work again, so Mike could
come back. Finally they got it
operating again.

Back in the house, Mike squealed as he tripped on a yellow rubber ducky and went rolling across the floor. When he came to a stop, Mike heard a lot of loud chuckles and giggles coming from down the hall.

Mike did not like this assignment—or this house, but he was determined to find the party. So, he lifted himself off the floor and followed the laughter.

But when he found the right door and opened it, there seemed to be nobody there.

Slowly, Mike entered the dark, quiet room. All of a sudden, a light went on! Mike jumped. He was surrounded by Shannon Brown and all her friends.

"Ahhhhhhhhh!" Mike let out the biggest scream in the history of screams! The girls roared with laughter at the little green monster.

At that exact moment, the door burst open, and

Sulley came barging through. Sulley was so surprised to find Mike screaming that all he could do

was let out an equally big scream. Then, Mike jumped right into Sulley's arms!

All of the girls at the slumber party laughed and laughed and laughed. A big blue monster with purple spots, hugging a one-eyed little green monster, was one of the funniest things they had ever seen. Mike and

Sulley caught their breath. Then they each took a bow.

"Looks as if our work here is done," Sulley said. He and Mike headed through the closet door and back to the Monsters, Inc., Laugh Floor. They had filled so many canisters that Mike met his laugh quota for the entire week.

"I wasn't scared for a second," said Mike, hoping Sulley would believe him.

"Me, neither, buddy," Sulley said, his big furry fingers crossed behind his back. "Me, neither."

Beautifully illustrated volumes filled with magical Disney stories

0-7868-3402-1

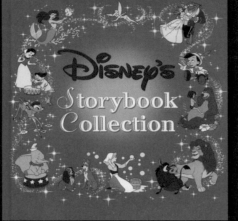

0-7868-3234-7

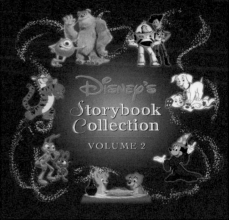

0-7868-3359-9

0-7868-3260-6

Collections for every family to treasure!

$15.99 each!
($19.99 CAN)

Collect Them All!

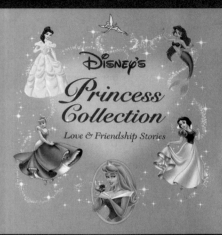

0-7868-3247-9

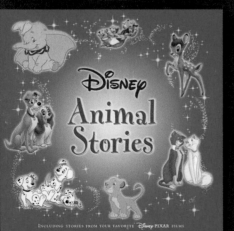

0-7868-3257-6

0-7868-3290-8

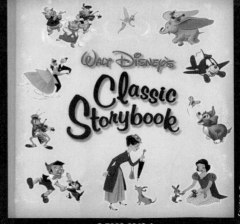

0-7868-3342-4

© Disney

 Visit us at www.disneybooks.com • Available at bookstores and retailers everywhere